ALASKAN GIRLS

Alaskan Girls

Summer Adventures

By Sam Britch

Indy Pub

CONTENTS

1 - Summer Plans 1

2 - The Hunt Begins 7

3 - Fishing Frenzy 12

4 - Time To Relax 19

5 - Gone Camping! 24

6 - Summer Is Over 36

1

SUMMER PLANS

Daisee and Abbee were sitting at the kitchen table when Dad walked in with a big grin on his face.

"Girls, I've got some plans for this summer," he said, setting a map down on the table.

Abbee's heart filled with excitement. She loved doing things with her dad and her little sister. "What kind of plans?" she asked eagerly.

Dad pointed to the map. "We're going to explore some new trails, find some great fishing spots, and maybe even go on a hunt or two."

Daisee's eyes widened. "Really? Can we bring Rocket and Ivan too?"

"Of course!" Dad replied, ruffling her hair. "They're part of the family, after all."

Abbee couldn't wait to get started. She loved the feeling of being out in the wilderness, surrounded by nature. Plus, spending time with her family made everything better. "When do we start?" she asked.

"Tomorrow morning," Dad said, checking his watch. "We've got a lot to do before we leave."

The girls grinned, already imagining all the adventures they would have. They couldn't wait to start exploring their beautiful home state of Alaska. This was going to be the best summer ever!

Ivan and Rocket were also ready to get started on their adventures; Sam had stocked up on supplies like food, outdoor gear, and maps. He checked the weather forecast for the Denali Highway one last time before loading everything into his truck.

Daisee and Abbee couldn't believe it-it felt like the summer had just begun but already they were about to embark on their first adventure. As Dad drove them out of town, they could see the sun setting over the mountains in the distance, and knew that it was going to be an amazing summer!

As they drove down the Denali Highway, Dad pointed out all the different wildlife and plants that lived in the area. The girls kept their eyes peeled for moose, bears, and other animals that called this place home. Soon enough, they reached a spot where Dad knew there was a good fishing hole-it was time to set up camp!

The girls got to work helping Dad pitch their tents while Ivan and Rocket eagerly explored the new territory.

With everything ready, they gathered around the fire to roast marshmallows and tell stories about what amazing things they would find on their journey ahead.

The summer had only just begun but already it was full of adventure! Daisee and Abbee couldn't wait to see what else the Denali Highway had in store for them. With Dad, Ivan, and Rocket by their side, they knew it was going to be an unforgettable summer!

The next morning, the sun shone brightly and the birds sang as Dad packed up camp. Daisee and Abbee were ready to continue their journey down the Denali Highway-what new adventures would they find today?

Only one way to find out...let the adventure begin! They set off on the hiking trail with a spirit of excitement and a sense of anticipation. With Dad, Ivan, and Rocket by their side, they knew they could conquer anything!

The Denali Highway was full of surprises-from beautiful mountains to hidden fishing spots, it had something for everyone. The sisters enjoyed spending time exploring the area and discovering its secrets. Whenever they came across an interesting sight or found a spot that looked like it would make a great place to camp, Dad would pull over so they could take in their surroundings.

Daisee and Abbee loved this way of life-it felt free and wild yet also comforting and familiar. They cherished every moment spent outside with their dad, Ivan, and Rocket by their side-the summer days flew by in a blur of adventure and exploration.

They finally made it to their fishing hole. Dad baited their hooks and cast out the line, hoping for a big catch. The girls were excited to see what they would pull in-it was always an adventure!

As sunset approached, Daisee and Abbee had caught a few fish, made some new bird friends, and learned a lot about nature and the outdoors. They enjoyed every second of it, feeling content knowing that there were more adventures to come on their journey down the Denali Highway.

The sun sank low in the sky as they hiked back to camp. Dad, Ivan and Rocket followed close behind as they traveled through the wilderness back to their tents.

The girls felt a sense of accomplishment knowing that they had conquered the Denali Highway on their first day!

2

THE HUNT BEGINS

The sisters awoke early the next morning-it was time to go hunting! Sam had packed their gear the night before, and now it was time to put it to use.

The group set off deep into the woods, with Dad leading the way and Ivan and Rocket following close behind. Daisee and Abbee were excited to finally be heading on their first hunting adventure!

The girls watched in awe as Dad taught them how to read the terrain and spot potential hunting spots. They were amazed at how knowledgeable he was about the area-it seemed as if he knew every nook and cranny of the woods.

Soon enough, they came across a spot that Dad thought looked promising. He instructed the girls to keep an eye out for the ever elusive caribou. The girls kept their eyes peeled, eagerly searching for any sign of movement.

Just as the sun was setting and they were about to give up, they heard a faint noise in the distance. Daisee and Abbee were elated-they had finally found their first caribou!

Sam asked both the girls who wanted to take the shot at the first caribou. After a few moments of deliberation, Daisee decided to take the shot. It was time for her to put all of that knowledge into practice.

Loading up her gun, she took aim and steadied herself, ready for the perfect shot. She slowly squeezed the trigger until there was a loud bang-she had hit her target! The caribou stumbled forward before dropping down lifelessly onto the ground. Daisee could hardly believe what she had done-she had just taken down her very first animal with her first shot! She looked over at Dad proudly as he praised her accomplishment.

The group gathered around their prize with respect and admiration for its beauty and strength. They thanked it for giving them sustenance before gathering up its remains so they could begin preparing dinner back at camp. As they hiked back through the woods, Daisee and Abbee felt a sense of pride for the success of their first hunting adventure.

The girls knew that this was only the beginning-they had lots more to learn and plenty more adventures awaiting them on their journey down the Denali Highway.

The night sky looked beautiful as the group started to clean the animal with dad. The night sky of the wilderness of the Denali Highway was full of wonders. As the sun set, the horizon was painted in brilliant hues of orange and pink. But as darkness fell, something else began to appear in the sky-the aurora borealis.

The sisters were mesmerized by this natural light show-the way it seemed to dance and swirl across the night sky was truly a sight to behold! The colors ranged from deep purples and blues to vibrant greens and pinks that illuminated their faces with an ethereal glow.

They had heard stories about how some lucky people have seen entire galaxies in these lights, but for now they were content just watching them undulate above them like waves on an ocean. They marveled at how delicate yet powerful these lights appeared as they moved through the air like ghostly apparitions.

As Ivan and Rocket chased each other around nearby trees, Daisee and Abbee sat back in awe of this mysterious phenomenon that had taken over their backyard for one magical evening. No matter how many times they witnessed it, nothing could compare to seeing these majestic lights dancing across the night sky!

It was definitely an evening that neither of them would forget!

The next morning, Daisee and Abbee awoke with a newfound appreciation for nature-the hunt had brought them closer together and taught them about the wilderness. They were excited for what their next adventure would bring!

The girls packed up their equipment, loaded the caribou into the truck, and made their way back to Anchorage. Although they had only been gone two days, it felt like an eternity-the sisters had definitely experienced a lot in that short amount of time.

They arrived back home and unloaded the caribou, feeling a sense of accomplishment that comes with a successful hunting and fishing trip. It had been an incredible journey, and the girls were excited to see what was in store for their next adventure!

3

FISHING FRENZY

After the girls had processed all the caribou, it was finally time to head out on their next adventure of the summer with dad. This time, they decided to head north to Fairbanks for another outdoor excursion.

They packed up their bags and set off on the road, looking forward to the beautiful scenery that awaited them. The drive was long but filled with breathtaking sights around every corner. They stopped for lunch at a quaint diner in Delta Junction, then continued along until they reached Fairbanks.

When they arrived at their destination, Sam was eager to get started. He took the girls on a short hike, then showed them some of his favorite spots for fishing and hunting. The sisters were excited to learn new skills and explore the great outdoors with their dad!

The next few days were spent out in nature, learning how to spot wildlife, build fires, and hunt and fish. Daisee and Abbee were growing more confident in their newfound skills, and were excited to put them to the test.

Since Daisee got to harvest the caribou, it was Abbee's turn to harvest. She wanted the biggest fish she could catch! After a few hours of fishing, they spotted a huge salmon swimming in the river. Abbee was determined to catch the biggest salmon she could find. She had been watching the river for hours, looking for any signs of movement in the water. Finally, her patience paid off when she spotted a huge king salmon swimming upstream!

She grabbed her fishing rod and cast out her line, hoping that this would be the one. Abbee held her breath as she watched anxiously for any sign of a bite. After what felt like an eternity, there it was-the telltale tug on the line that signaled a fish had taken hold! Her rod bent nearly in half!

With all her strength and focus, Abbee worked to reel in the large fish from its home in the depths of the river. The battle between man and nature seemed never ending as she fought against time and exhaustion to bring it closer and closer to shore. Finally, after much effort and determination, Abbee managed to land her prize-a magnificent 25 pound salmon! Sam had been watching Abbee intently, marveling at her determination and skill as she battled against the large salmon.

He was proud of his daughter for tackling this challenge head-on and giving it her all, despite the odds being stacked against her.

He knew that landing a fish like this one would take patience and strength, both of which he could see in his daughter's eyes. So when the moment finally arrived where Abbee needed a helping hand to bring the fish ashore, Sam stepped in without hesitation to lend a hand. Together they worked together until their prize was finally landed!

The two were ecstatic with their success-Abbee couldn't believe she had actually managed to catch such a huge fish on her own! She beamed with pride as Sam praised her for doing such an impressive job and thanked him for his help along the way. It felt great knowing that they had accomplished something so special together! They took lots of photos of the trophy salmon.

Daisee was so proud of her sister and couldn't help but show her affections. She leaned in and kissed the fish right on the lips! Then helped her clean the large salmon. With Sam's guidance and some teamwork, the sisters managed to gut the fish, remove its scales, and even slice it into steaks for dinner.

The sisters eagerly helped their dad set up his portable smoker so that they could smoke the fish for dinner. They carefully measured out the wood chips and placed them in the smoker, following instructions from Sam. With a few minor adjustments, they got the fire going and soon had the aroma of smoked salmon filling the air around them. Abbee was so proud of herself for managing to catch such a huge fish and felt like she really did belong in this beautiful, remote part of Alaska with her dad and sister.

After dinner was ready, the three of them settled down around the fire and enjoyed their meal together. It had been a long day out exploring nature and Abbee was feeling content . She knew that she had found a peace out here in the backcountry and was glad to be able to share this experience with her family.

The sisters' adventures of fishing, hunting, and exploring were just beginning, and they couldn't wait to see what other surprises nature held in store for them! With Ivan and Rocket by their side, Abbee and Daisee had a feeling it would be quite the adventure! From that day forward, they knew that Alaska would always be their home.

The girls and dad settled into their tent with full bellies and their furry sidekicks keeping guard. Dad unzipped the roof of the tent so the girls could marvel at the stars in the night sky.

The night sky was alive with color and light as the aurora borealis lit up the landscape around Abbee, Daisee and their dad. They were so excited to see such an incredible display of nature's beauty again! The shimmering hues of purple, pink, green, blue and yellow cast an ethereal glow across the sky, and the trio were filled with a sense of wonder.

With contentment in their hearts, the three said good night and drifted off to sleep beneath the stars, dreaming of tomorrow's adventures.

The next morning, the three awoke to a beautiful sunrise. After grabbing some breakfast, they began to break camp and prepare for their return trip back home to Anchorage. Sam was in charge of packing up all the gear while Abbee and Daisee helped him out by making sure nothing was left behind. They worked together quickly yet efficiently, folding up tents, stowing away sleeping bags and blankets, and gathering any stray items that might have been forgotten the night before. The girls also made sure Ivan and Rocket were ready for travel as well!

When everything had been packed up, the family loaded their gear into Sam's truck and hit the road. As they drove away from the backcountry, Abbee and Daisee looked out at the beautiful landscape they were leaving behind. They felt satisfied knowing that they had experienced an amazing adventure together and couldn't wait to return soon!

The drive home from Fairbanks was a long but enjoyable one. As they made their way along the winding roads, Abbee and Daisee watched as the landscape changed from lush green forests to snow-capped mountains and then to wide open plains. They marveled at the breathtaking beauty of the Alaskan wilderness, feeling grateful to call this wild place home.

Eventually, the family arrived back in Anchorage, tired but happy and full of stories from their adventure! The sisters felt rejuvenated and excited to plan their next outdoor excursion. With Sam's guidance and some teamwork, they knew they could tackle any challenge that nature threw at them!

4

TIME TO RELAX

The girls had already had a very adventerous summer. The week after they got back from their epic fishing journey, they decided to have a relaxing week.

Abbee and Daisee had a plan! With help from their dad, Sam, they were going to set up a lemonade stand in front of their house. They just needed to come up with the perfect recipe for their homemade lemonade.

The girls worked together in the kitchen of their small home in Anchorage to create their delicious concoction. After tasting the finished product, they were both pleased with the results! Now all they had to do was set up their stand and start selling.

With a little help from Sam, the girls put together a cute little display for their lemonade stand. They hung a sign that read "Abbee & Daisee's Lemonade Stand – Coldest Drinks In Town!" and set up a few chairs for customers to sit in while they enjoyed their refreshments.

The sisters were ready to get started! Throughout the day, more and more people stopped by to buy glasses of freshly-made lemonade. Everyone was delighted with Abbee and Daisee's sweet and tangy beverage, and by the end of the day they had earned enough money to buy themselves a celebratory treat.

The lemonade stand was a success! Abbee and Daisee learned a lot about business, but also enjoyed some much-deserved rest. They had such a good time that they wanted to have another sale! This time, Daisee had the great idea of baking cookies to sell alongside the lemonade. Their dad had taught Abbee how to make some delicious cookies recently, so Abbee got right to work!

Abbee was excited to put her baking skills to the test. She had been learning how to bake from her dad and now she was ready to try it out for herself. She decided that chocolate chip and snickerdoodle cookies would be perfect for their next lemonade stand sale, as they were sure to please all of their customers!

Abbee preheated the oven, grabbed a mixing bowl, and began gathering all of the ingredients she needed: butter, sugar, eggs, flour, vanilla extract and of course some chocolate chips. With a few quick steps she mixed together everything into a thick cookie dough. Then came time for rolling out the dough into individual balls which Abbee placed onto two greased baking sheets. Finally it was time to pop them in the oven!

Next up were Daisee's favorite - Snickerdoodles! For these cookies Abbee used much of same ingredients but replaced some with cream cheese instead of butter and added cinnamon powder too. Again Abbee rolled out small balls of dough before placing them on two separate trays ready for baking in the oven alongside her chocolate chip cookies. As soon as they went in Abbee could smell an amazing aroma filling up the kitchen.

Daisee was eagerly waiting for the snickerdoodles to come out of the oven. She had been helping Abbee with all of the preparation and now she couldn't wait to get her hands on them! As soon as they were done baking, Daisee quickly grabbed a bowl and mixed together some cinnamon powder, sugar and butter until it formed a thick paste-like consistency. With excitement in her eyes, Daisee took each cookie off of the pan one by one and carefully spooned some of this topping onto each one before setting them aside. Finally, after what seemed like forever, all of their hard work was finally complete - Abbee's delicious chocolate chip cookies alongside Daisee's special snickerdoodle cinnamon treats!

The girls set their lemonade stand back up at the end of the driveway. Abbee and Daisee were thrilled with the success of their second lemonade and cookie stand! They had created a product that people could not resist. Everyone in town was talking about Abbee and Daisee's delicious creations, so much so that customers started to line up at their door just for a taste. With each passing day, more and more people came out to get some of the best baked goods in Anchorage!Abbee and Daisee's lemonade stand was a huge success, with customers lining up to get their hands on the delicious treats they had created.

The sisters were thrilled with how much money they made from the sale of their goods, and decided to spend it on something special. With their earnings, they decided to take the whole family on a trip to Denali National Park so they could really explore Alaska and all of its beauty.

5

GONE CAMPING!

Abbee and Daisee were excited to embark on another adventure. After selling their delicious treats at the lemonade stand, they had saved up enough money for a camping trip with their dad and two dogs, Ivan and Rocket. They spent days packing all of the necessary items for the long journey ahead: food, clothes, camping gear, sleeping bags - you name it!

Finally ready to go, Abbee and Daisee hopped into the car with Sam and their two furry friends as they set off on an epic road trip up to Denali National Park. Abbee and Daisee were filled with excitement as they drove north towards Denali National Park. They had been looking forward to this adventure for weeks, and now the time had finally come! As they journeyed further up the winding roads, their anticipation only grew as breathtaking views of snow-covered mountains passed by their car window. The sisters could hardly believe that such a beautiful place existed right in their own backyard. Nothing could have prepared them for what lay ahead - an unforgettable experience full of fun, exploration and discovery!

The drive was long but it was worth it − every twist in the road revealed more stunning scenery than before. Abbee and Daisee watched in awe as majestic mountain peaks stretched out into the horizon while lush green forests surrounded them on either side.

Every so often they would catch a glimpse of wild-life too – from moose grazing along the roadside to bald eagles soaring high above them against a back-drop of bright blue sky.

After hours spent driving through never ending wilderness, Abbee and Daisee eventually arrived at Denali National Park just after sunset. It was already dark outside, but the sisters were still able to make out the silhouette of Denali's highest peak against a star-studded night sky. They had never seen anything so beautiful before and couldn't wait for the sun to rise tomorrow so they could explore this incredible landscape. With excitement in their hearts, they set up camp and laid under the stars.

The dark of night had settled over the camp as Abbee and Daisee slept peacefully in their tents. Suddenly, their slumber was broken by a loud rustling outside. Startled, they both awoke and raced out to investigate the source of the commotion.

Much to their surprise, a black bear had wandered into camp and was rummaging through their belong-ings! With heart pounding in fear, the sisters quickly retreated back into their tents while dad Sam grabbed a flashlight and shined it at the bear. But instead of being frightened away, the bear only seemed more interested as it moved closer towards them!

With no other option, Sam bravely yelled at the bear in an attempt to scare it away from camp. Thankfully, it worked – the bear soon scurried off into the nearby woods with Ivan and Rocket following close behind. After a few tense moments of silence, everyone let out a collective sigh of relief as Dad reassured his daughters that everything was going to be okay.

Although shaken up by the incident, Abbee and Daisee couldn't help but feel excited after seeing a wild animal up close like that! It was definitely not something you see everyday! Once they were all calmed down again, they sat around the campfire talking about what an incredible experience they'd just shared together – one they would never forget!

The next morning, Sam asked Abbee and Daisee what they wanted to do. They told him all the things they had been looking forward to: hiking through the mountains, fishing in the lake, and learning more about the local wildlife. Sam smiled knowingly, he was just as excited to explore Denali National Park with his two daughters as they were!

Early that morning, Abbee and Daisee started packing backpacks full of snacks, water bottles and coats for their first day-long adventure. After a quick breakfast of hot oatmeal and fresh blueberry muffins, they were out the door with Ivan and Rocket leading the way.

The sisters spent hours exploring the national park - from trekking along rocky trails to fishing in rivers and lakes. Everywhere they looked there was something new to discover! As they hiked through meadows filled with wildflowers, Daisee spotted a family of mountain goats perched atop a jagged cliff face far off in the distance. She quickly grabbed her binoculars for a closer look while Abbee snapped photos of them with her camera.

When lunchtime came around, Sam set up a picnic spot by a picturesque riverbank where everyone could relax and enjoy some food together before continuing on their journey. After lunch they went on one last hike - this time it was up to a nearby lookout where they could get an amazing view of Denali's highest peak rising up above them like a snow-capped giant. With tired legs but content hearts, everyone made their way back down the mountain and headed back to camp for dinner at sunset.

It had been an incredible day full of memories that would stay with Abbee and Daisee forever. As night fell over Denali National Park, thoughts of their adventures kept both sisters dreaming until morning light once again illuminated the landscape outside their window.

The next morning, it was time for another adventure. This time, dad had a surprise for the girls. He had brought some inflatable canoes for the girls as a surprise. While the girls were still sleeping, he pumped up the boats and got them ready.

Later in the morning, Abbee and Daisee were awoken by the bright morning sun streaming through their tent window. Rubbing their eyes sleepily, they stepped outside to find dad Sam standing there with two large inflatable canoes tucked under his arms. With a proud smile on his face, he revealed that he had set these up for their next adventure!

The sisters couldn't believe their eyes - not only did they get to go on a canoe trip, but it was also an unexpected surprise from Dad! They quickly changed out of their pajamas and helped Dad fill the boats with the life jackets and paddles that he had also prepared for them. With one last wave goodbye, the sisters hopped into the boats and started paddling away down the river.

The crisp morning air felt refreshing against Abbee and Daisee's faces as they glided effortlessly along the water's edge. As they rounded each bend in the river, new scenery awaited them - snow-capped mountains reflected against smooth glassy waters with countless wildflowers dotting the shoreline like stars in a night sky. The three of them savored every moment of this peaceful voyage, soaking in all that beauty around them while creating wonderful memories together.

Eventually, they reached a spot that was perfect for stopping and having some lunch before heading back home. After lunch was over, everyone packed up their things and started heading back down-river towards camp at a more leisurely pace than before – enjoying each other's company as well as nature's untouched beauty in all its glory.

As they reached camp again, Abbee and Daisee looked back at their day spent on the river with fondness; it was one of those days where everything just seems to click into place perfectly - from Dad's surprise canoes to spending time with one another surrounded by nature's wonders - making this canoe trip an unforgettable memory that will stay with both girls forever.

The girls had so much fun the previous day that they asked to go on the boats again!

The morning sun shone brightly as Abbee and Daisee launched their inflatable kayaks onto the lake. Together, they paddled with enthusiasm, exploring every nook and cranny of the lake. As they navigated around boulders and weaved through wild reeds, Dad rowed nearby in his own kayak, watching his daughters with pride. Ivan and Rocket followed close behind, swimming alongside the boats while barking excitedly.

On their journey around the lake, Abbee and Daisee discovered an old tree branch jutting out from the water. With a little help from Dad Sam, they managed to pull it out from beneath the surface. They then proceeded to build a makeshift raft by stacking up all of their belongings on top of it - including food supplies, sleeping bags and extra clothes for warmth - before pushing it back into the water once again.

With Dad leading the way in his kayak at the front of the convoy, Abbee and Daisee took turns rowing their makeshift raft through choppy waves while Ivan and Rocket kept pace beside them beneath the surface of the lake. As they glided across its shimmering waters, they couldn't help but feel awestruck by nature's beauty all around them.

The sun beamed down from above while fish splashed in one direction and birds flew in another – it was a perfect moment!

Finally reaching a small island near the middle of lake, everyone pulled up to shore for a much-needed break. They set up camp on sandy beach as dad cooked up some hot dogs over an open fire for lunch before everyone settled down for siesta time amongst towering evergreens trees that provided just enough shade from afternoon sunrays.

Afterwards, Abbee and Daisee decided to take some initiative by gathering rocks to form a cairn on top of island which would serve as a marker so other adventurers could know where they had been. Afterwards Dad decided it was time for swimming – so after stripping off their clothes he lead everyone into cold water below until even Ivan jumped in! For hours they swam together among colorful schools of fish while making jokes about who could hold their breath underwater longer!

As night fell over lake, group returned to shore where Dad cooked dinner over fire once again before settling down into sleeping bags early that night.

Despite being exhausted from such an adventurous day playing on Butte Lake, both sisters drifted off feeling happy – grateful for having had such an incredible experience with family deep in Alaskan wilderness!

The next morning, it was time to break camp and head back to Anchorage. Abbee and Daisee said goodbye to the wilderness and set off for their journey back home. Dad Sam drove them in his truck while Ivan and Rocket rode along in the back – excited as ever!

The drive was uneventful but pleasant; they passed through rolling hills of green forests that seemed to stretch out forever beneath a sunny sky. As they got closer to Anchorage, Dad decided it would be fun to make one last stop before heading home: an ice cream parlor at the edge of town! Everyone agreed this was a great idea so with smiles on their faces, they all piled out of car ready for some delicious treats.

At first, both sisters were overwhelmed by sheer variety flavors available – from classic vanilla bean to exotic mango sorbet - making it difficult for them choose just one scoop each! In the end though, Abbee opted for double-chocolate chip while Daisee went with mint chocolate swirl - both topped off with rainbow sprinkles of course.

They then found seats outside where everyone could sit together enjoying summer breeze as well as each other's company while savoring every lick of their cold creamy desserts. Soon enough however, it was time to go home and soon enough the whole family - along with Ivan and Rocket - were back in Anchorage planning their next adventure!

It had been an incredible journey packed full of excitement, learning, laughter and love. As they drove away the girls knew they would never forget this special day – forever treasuring memories made in wild Alaskan wilderness.

Surely there would be many more unforgettable adventures ahead...but for now, Abbee and Daisee could look forward to coming home and sharing stories about their latest outing with friends – heads high with pride as true Alaskan adventurers!

Abbee and Daisee had been looking forward to coming home ever since they left on their Alaskan adventure. As soon as Dad Sam pulled up in his truck, the girls jumped out with Ivan and Rocket excitedly barking along with them. They were so ready to tell everyone about their amazing journey! But first, they had to help unpack the car from all of their supplies. So without further ado, the sisters set off to lend a hand.

Once everything was unloaded and put away, they regrouped in the living room to share stories about their adventure. Dad Sam began by recounting a few of his own experiences like how he caught a giant fish off the shore of Butte Lake or how he found that mysterious old rope swing in the woods behind camp. Then Abbee and Daisee jumped in with tales of their own about swimming with schools of colorful fish or building a cairn on top of an island. As each story was shared, everyone launched into laughter – all having had such an incredible time during their Alaskan escapade!

When the stories were done, it was finally time for rest...and what better way to end such a wonderful day than by snuggling up with Ivan and Rocket - both exhausted from all the adventures but happy to be home.

Soon enough, everyone was fast asleep dreaming of their next great Alaskan adventure....

6

SUMMER IS OVER

With summer coming to an end, Abbee and Daisee had one week left to relax before school started again. They spent the days exploring their backyard, playing with Ivan and Rocket, and soaking up the last few moments of summertime bliss. Each day was filled with laughter as they ran around in circles chasing each other or just lounging in a hammock enjoying some peace and quiet. But most importantly, it was time for them to make lasting memories that would carry them through the long winter months ahead.

The girls knew they needed to prep their chickens for the upcoming fall and winter season.

The girls had their work cut out for them when it came to tending to their five chickens. Every morning and evening, Abbee and Daisee would head out to the chicken coop located in the far corner of their back-yard. Sam had built it himself, with the intention of giving his daughters a chance to learn responsibility while also providing them with some much-needed fresh eggs!

Once they reached the coop, they'd quickly gather eggs in a basket that hung on the wall before check-ing on each individual chicken. The sisters would take turns brushing away dirt and feathers from each bird's back as well as spraying down any areas that looked particularly dry or scaly.

They also made sure there was plenty of food and water for the chickens throughout the day, getting creative with scavenging leftovers from meals gone by!

But perhaps most importantly, Abbee and Daisee showed their chickens an immense amount of love every single day. They'd talk softly to each one as if they were old friends and spend extra time cuddling with them during cold Alaskan evenings. As summer turned into fall, this routine only seemed to become more important: like having a little bit of sunshine in the midst of autumn chill. The bond between the birds and girls was undeniable - providing them both with comfort and companionship during these long Alaskan days.

Sam had always been proud of Abbee and Daisee - ever since the day they were born. They were his everything, and he made sure to teach them important life lessons and values as they grew up. But now that they were in their teenage years, he was especially proud of the young women they had become. Not only had they taken on responsibility with helping out around the house, but they had also embraced adventure with such grace and tenacity.

Sam watched as both girls took charge of their own backyard projects - from tending to the chickens to building a cairn on an island – and it filled him with joy knowing that his daughters were growing into confident young adults.

Sam was also impressed by how well-rounded Abbee and Daisee had become during their summer adventures in Alaska. The sisters had gone beyond just outdoor exploration; they found themselves learning about local ecosystems, learning new survival skills, and even cooking over a campfire! They even managed to make friends with residents along their travels, which was no small feat considering how long summer days can be in Alaska! To Sam, these experiences showed him that his daughters could handle anything life threw at them - both good and bad - with intelligence and poise.

He felt so fortunate to have such wonderful girls by his side as he watched them blossom into strong women. He knew deep down that his daughters would continue to take on more challenging endeavors in the future, all while keeping their hearts full of kindness and love for one another. Sam couldn't help but smile when he thought about the incredible people Abbee and Daisee were becoming – two young Alaskan adventurers who were continuously pushing outside of their comfort zones...just like him.

www.ingramcontent.com/pod-product-compliance
Lightning Source LLC
Chambersburg PA
CBHW051002060726
47593CB00018B/2373